A Lucky Charm
My Special Heart

by Marcy Merriwether
Illustrated by Jael

kidsbooks
Incorporated

Bethany and Sara stood side by side in the busy airport waiting room. The two girls held hands, but they didn't speak. They were afraid that if they did, they would cry. They were best friends, but today was the last day they would be together. Sara and her family were moving.

The two girls had lived in the same town all their lives. They grew up together. They went to the same school and even had the same teachers. Now they would be separated

for the first time. It wasn't an ordinary good-bye, like when Bethany visited her aunt one summer, or when Sara spent a week on her grandfather's farm. This time, the whole Atlantic Ocean would be between them. Sara's father had been transferred to England. Today Sara and her mother would fly there to join him. Sara would be gone, and Bethany would lose the best friend she ever had.

The two girls stood near a boarding gate with their mothers. The airport hummed with activity as passengers hurried to catch their flights or were greeted by happy shouts and smiles. Mrs. Bradford, Bethany's mother, chatted quietly with Mrs. Webster. But the two young friends paid no attention to any of it, as they stood quietly holding hands. It was the saddest day of their lives.

"Attention passengers. International flight 101 for London is now boarding at gate seven." The announcer's voice was calm and reassuring, but it brought chills to the small group standing near the gate.

Mrs. Bradford touched her daughter's arm. "It's time to leave, Bethany," she said softly. She took her hand. "I'm sorry."

"Just a few more minutes, Mom," Bethany said.

"It's not up to me," Mrs. Bradford said sadly. She turned to Mrs. Webster. "We're going to miss you two very much," she said.

"We'll miss you, too," Sara's mother said. "But I know Sara and Bethany will keep the post office busy. And so will I. I promise."

AIR EUROPE
NOW BOARDING

She glanced at her wristwatch and then at the girls. "I guess we have another minute," she said.

The two mothers stepped back so the girls could be alone. "I don't know what they'll do without one another," Mrs. Webster said. "They've known each other since they were babies."

Bethany's mother smiled. "I know," she said. "They're just like sisters."

"That's what's going to make it so hard for everyone," Mrs. Webster said, checking her watch again.

The loudspeaker crackled. "Last call for passengers boarding international flight 101," the announcer said. This time the voice boomed like thunder through the crowded waiting room. "All passengers for London must now board. Last call."

Bethany and Sara couldn't hold back their sadness any longer. Teardrops ran down their cheeks in salty streaks. They threw their arms around one another and squeezed. They held on to each other so tightly it was hard to tell where one girl ended and the other began. "You'll always be my best friend no matter where I live," Sara said.

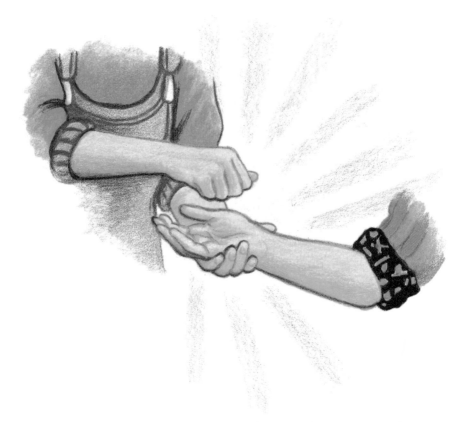

"And you'll always be my best friend, too," Bethany said. "Forever!"

Mrs. Webster took Sara's hand and squeezed it gently.

Sara glanced up. "Just one more minute, Mom," she pleaded.

Mrs. Webster shook her head from side to side. "It's time," she said. "We have to go."

Sara and her mother turned toward the door leading to the airplane. Sara hadn't gone three steps when she pulled her hand from her mother's grip. She ran back to Bethany. She opened the small purse she carried and stuck her hand inside. When she pulled it out, her hand was closed in a tight fist. She put her hand in Bethany's. "This is for you," she said. "I almost forgot." Sara opened her fist and dropped a small object into Bethany's palm. "It's the most special thing I own. It means you'll always have a friend." She hugged Bethany one last time. Then she quickly turned and ran back to join her mother. The two stepped through the door and vanished.

Bethany and her mother joined the crowd leaving the waiting room. They walked silently into the warm, morning sunshine and went to their car. Bethany climbed into the

front seat and buckled up. She stared blankly out the window. Her right hand was tightly clenched into a fist. She didn't say a word all the way home.

The moment she stopped the car in their driveway, Mrs. Bradford turned to her daughter. "I wish there were something I could say, darling. I know how hard it is to say good-bye." She stroked Bethany's long brown hair. "But you'll find another best friend. I promise."

Bethany couldn't hold back any longer. She threw her arms around her mother's neck and started to cry out loud. "Oh, Mom!" she sobbed. "How could anybody ever be as good a friend as Sara?"

"Perhaps it's just one of those things we'll have to wait and see about," she said.

Bethany raised her head. Her nose was red, and salty tears streaked her face. "Do you think so?" she asked. She rubbed her nose with the back of her hand. She suddenly stopped to stare at her closed fist. She had completely forgotten. She opened the hand slowly. "Oh!" she gasped. "Look!"

Lying in the center of her palm like a precious piece of lost treasure was a small gold heart attached to a short gold chain. The heart was as shiny as a brand-new penny and the bracelet sparkled in the cheery sunlight. "It's the special friendship heart I gave to Sara!" Bethany exclaimed. "It's her favorite piece of jewelry in the whole world."

"Oh, yes!" Mrs. Bradford exclaimed. "I remember. You gave it to Sara as a sign of your friendship."

"It stands for true friends," Bethany said excitedly. "You give it to the person you know will be your friend forever, no matter what happens." Her face brightened. She pressed the heart to her chest, close to her own. Then the memory of the sad parting tugged at her once again. Her face clouded over. Fresh tears ran like raindrops down her

cheeks. She sobbed and couldn't speak.

"It was the nicest thing she could do," Mrs. Bradford said as they walked to the house. "By giving it back to you, she was saying she will always be your friend."

"That's what a special heart bracelet means," Bethany said with a smile. "That's why you give it to someone. To have them for a friend. Forever. No matter what."

Mrs. Bradford led the way to the kitchen. She was happy to see Bethany smiling again. "Give me your arm," she said brightly. "Let's see how your special heart fits."

Bethany handed the special gold heart to her mother and put out her arm.

Mrs. Bradford held the ends with the tips of her fingers as if the bracelet were the most precious thing in the world. She slipped it over Bethany's wrist and closed the clasp

with a solid *click*. "Ah!" Mrs. Bradford said.
"Perfect! It's as if it were made for you."

"It was!" Bethany exclaimed. "It was
made for special friends, and I'm Sara's
special friend, just like she's mine." The heart
dangled from her arm, sparkling like a tiny
jewel. She glanced at her mother. "It brings
friends together, even when there's an ocean
between them."

"I think you're right," Mrs. Bradford said.

"I'll never take it off," Bethany said. She was still smiling. "I'm going to wear it forever!"

Bethany didn't remove the bracelet that night when she went to bed. It was still on her wrist the next morning when she woke up. It swung from her arm every day after that, a happy reminder that she had a best friend. She wore it to school and she wore it at play. But sometimes when she stopped to look at the special heart, she felt sad. It reminded her that Sara was far away.

"I wish I had a friend like Sara right here," Bethany said one spring day when she was feeling especially sad. "We live so far from everyone, I don't know what I'm going to do when summer comes and school is out."

The Bradford's house was in the country. Neighbors were few and far between. Thick woods filled the countryside. It was a beautiful place to live, and Bethany loved it. She spent hours roaming the woods and meadows. The country was tons of fun, but it could be lonely, too.

The next two months passed quickly. Summer vacation would begin soon and Bethany was lonelier than ever. She spent hours in her backyard reading and daydreaming. Sometimes she thought about Sara, but it only made her sad.

One day Bethany poked her head into the kitchen. "I'm going to look for wildflowers in the woods," she said.

"What a good idea!" Mrs. Bradford said. "Just look out for poison ivy." She watched her daughter trudge into the woods. She shook her head. "Oh, Sara," she sighed. "You have no idea how much she misses you. I wish..."

Just then the phone rang and she forgot what she was thinking.

Birds chirped and squirrels chattered noisily as Bethany wandered deep into the woods picking flowers. She rested on an old stump by a small brook to watch the frogs. Afterwards, she crossed a grassy meadow and stirred up bugs that filled the air with buzzing.

When Bethany reached the big hill on the far side of the woods, she stopped. She had never been on the other side of the hill. She didn't know what was there.

Bethany looked at the hill for a while and then sadly turned around to go home. Summer would be no fun without a friend.

When Bethany reached her yard, she was streaked with grime from her hike. Her sneakers were covered with mud, and bits of twigs and leaves dotted her hair like little ribbons.

"My goodness," Mrs. Bradford said as Bethany stepped into the kitchen. "Look at what the cat dragged in. You'd better jump out of those things and take a bath or another cat might drag you right back out."

Bethany smiled and went to her room.

A moment later a scream startled Mrs. Bradford right down to her bones. It came from Bethany's room. She raced up the stairs. "Bethany! What's the matter?" she shouted.

Bethany stood in the middle of her room, looking completely stunned. "My special heart!" she cried. She held up her bare arm. It was streaked with dirt, but there was no bracelet. "It's gone!"

Mrs. Bradford took Bethany into her arms to console her. "We'll find it," she said. "Put your shoes back on and come with me."

The two searched the woods. They searched the meadow. They retraced every step of Bethany's hike. But they did not find

the special heart. It was truly gone.

Bethany was heartbroken. She sat in her room all the next day. Nothing her mother said or did could make up for the lost bracelet and everything it meant.

"It's going to be a very long summer," Mrs. Bradford sighed as she watched Bethany while away the hours. "A very long, lonely summer without a friend."

Maggie Tippet's mother stuck her head out the kitchen door. "It's time to come in, Maggie," she called.

Maggie sat cross-legged on the grass in her backyard. She put her finger to her lips. "Sssh, Mom," she shushed, as she pointed to a nearby tree. A small gray bird hopped from branch to branch. It held a long piece of dried grass in its beak.

Mrs. Tippet walked softly into the yard.

"She's building a new nest," Maggie whispered. "Look."

The bird flew off. It shot into the sky and disappeared over the big hill behind the Tippet's property. Mrs. Tippet sat on the grass next to her young daughter. They waited. Soon the bird reappeared. This time it carried something in its beak that sparkled like a tiny mirror.

"Look!" Maggie said softly. "It found something shiny."

Mother and daughter watched in wonder as the bird carefully tucked the shiny object into its nest. The moment it flew off for more nest-building material, Maggie leaped to her feet and raced to the tree. She quickly climbed up to the branch holding the newly built nest and peered in. "Oh, wow!" she exclaimed. She gingerly reached into the nest so she would not disturb the bird's work and then slid down the tree to the ground. She ran straight to her mother.

"A bracelet!" Maggie cried excitedly. "A gold bracelet with a shiny gold heart!" She held up the bracelet to show her mother her

treasure. "The clasp is broken, but otherwise it's just perfect!" She wrapped the chain around her wrist. "And it fits like it was made specially for me!"

Mrs. Tippet took the bracelet for a closer look. "This will be easy to fix," she said, shaking her head in amazement. "Somebody must have lost it, but who could it be?"

Later that week, Maggie and her mom were at the supermarket shopping for groceries. The golden charm dangled from Maggie's wrist.

"I'll meet you at the checkout counter," Mrs. Tippet said. "It may take a while. I still have to learn where everything is in this store." The Tippets were new in town. Even grocery shopping was an adventure. Mrs. Tippet pushed her cart down an aisle and was gone.

Maggie wandered up one aisle and down another. She stopped at the magazine rack. A girl her age sat on the lower shelf flipping through magazines. The girl didn't notice her. Maggie took down a magazine and looked at it for a few moments. When she put it back on the rack, it fell to the floor. The girl picked up the magazine and handed it to Maggie.

"Thanks," Maggie said. The two girls' hands nearly touched. The girl gasped, but Maggie didn't notice. She was already on her way to another part of the store.

A little later, on the opposite side of the market, Maggie heard footsteps behind her. She glanced over her shoulder. The girl from the magazine rack was at the end of the aisle. The instant Maggie saw her, the girl popped out of sight. The girl was there again when Maggie went to the checkout counter to meet her mom. When the girl saw that Maggie was going to leave the store, she vanished.

Maggie mentioned the girl to her mother as they walked across the parking lot to their car. "It was the weirdest thing," Maggie said. "She kept staring at me."

"Maybe she recognized you," Mrs. Tippett said.

"How could she?" Maggie answered. "I don't know anybody here yet. Besides, I never even saw her before."

Mrs. Tippet put the groceries into the car. "I'm sorry I didn't see her," she said.

Maggie put her hand on her mother's arm. "Well, it's not too late," she whispered. "There she is again!"

"That girl?" Maggie's mother asked, pointing across the parking lot. A young girl and a woman approached the Tippet's car.

"Yes!" Maggie said. "She's the one!"

The woman and the girl walked straight to the Tippets. The woman was smiling, but the girl's face was very serious. They stopped when they reached the Tippet's car. The girl stayed in the woman's shadow.

"Excuse me. I hope you'll forgive us," the woman said. "You see, my daughter noticed your daughter's bracelet and…"

The girl stepped forward. Her eyes were on the charm on Maggie's wrist. Her serious look fell away. In its place was the sad look of a lonely little girl. "I used to have one just like it," she said quietly. "It was a friendship heart. It was a present I gave to my best friend. She gave it back to me this year because she was moving away. It means you're friends forever. Then I lost it and…"

The girl's voice choked. She knew if she said one more word, she would start to cry.

Maggie's face brightened into a wide smile. She held up the bracelet so it caught the sunlight. It sparkled as if it were on fire. "And I found it," she shouted with delight.

Bethany's eyes opened wide. "You mean you found that bracelet?" she asked.

"Yes!" Maggie exclaimed. "And do you know how? You'll never believe it!"

"Do you think it could be…" Bethany was so excited she couldn't speak.

"Yours?" Maggie said, finishing what Bethany wanted to say. "It could be. Let me tell you how I found it." She stepped very close to Bethany and spoke as if she were telling a deep secret. "You see, we just moved to town this summer. We live in a house way out in the country. There's nothing there but a lot of woods and a big hill."

"A big hill?" Bethany said. "We've got a big hill behind our house, too! But I never knew what was on the other side."

"Well, I know what's on the other side," Maggie said, pointing to herself. "Me!" She quickly slipped the bracelet off her wrist and clasped it on Bethany's wrist before Bethany could say a word.

The two mothers smiled at one another, and introduced themselves and their daughters.

"I think we should go somewhere and talk," Bethany's mom said.

"I certainly agree with that," Maggie's mom replied. She turned to the girls. "What do you two think?" They were already on their way to the ice-cream parlor next to the market. The charm glittered from Bethany's wrist like a tiny beacon of friendship.

The two mothers and their daughters sat around a table in the ice-cream parlor. While the women got to know each other, the two girls rambled on like old friends.

"We'll be in the same grade," Bethany said excitedly.

"With the same teacher!" Maggie exclaimed.

Bethany suddenly became very quiet.

"Is something wrong?" Maggie asked.

"I was just thinking," Bethany said. "I gave this bracelet to Sara, my best friend, and she gave it to her best friend, me." She held up her wrist so they could both see the lucky charm. "Maybe I didn't really lose my special heart in the woods. Maybe I was giving it to you. I just didn't know you were there yet, that's all."

"And I gave it back," Maggie said. "If a special friendship can cross a whole ocean, that old hill sure isn't going to keep us apart."

"Imagine," Maggie's mother said to Bethany's mother, "we could have lived on the other side of that hill all summer and never known we had neighbors."

"I wouldn't be so sure about that," Bethany's mother said. "I think there's something extra special about that gold heart and friendship. It seems to bring good friends together, and then it keeps them together."

Bethany smiled brightly. The bracelet once again dangled happily from her wrist. "It is special," she said. "It's my very special heart."